Visit us at www.abdopublishing.com

Reinforced library bound edition published in 2013 by Spotlight, a division of the ABDO Group, PO Box 398166, Minneapolis, MN 55439. Spotlight produces high-quality reinforced library bound editions for schools and libraries. Published by agreement with Warner Bros.-A Time Warner Company.
Printed in the United States of America, North Mankato, Minnesota.
102012
012013

♻ This book contains at least 10% recycled materials.

Library of Congress Cataloging-in-Publication Data

Rozum, John.
 Scooby-Doo in Yankee Doodle danger / writer, John Rozum ; artist, Fabio Laguna. -- Reinforced library bound edition.
    pages cm. -- (Scooby-Doo graphic novels)
 ISBN 978-1-61479-054-9
 1. Graphic novels. I. Laguna, Fabio, illustrator. II. Scooby-Doo (Television program) III. Title. IV. Title: Yankee Doodle danger.
 PZ7.7.R69Sc 2013
 741.5'973--dc23
                                        2012033329

All Spotlight books are reinforced library bindings
and manufactured in the United States of America.

SCOOBY-DOO!

Table of Contents

YANKEE DOODLE DANGER 4

FROM RUSSIA WITH GLOVE 14

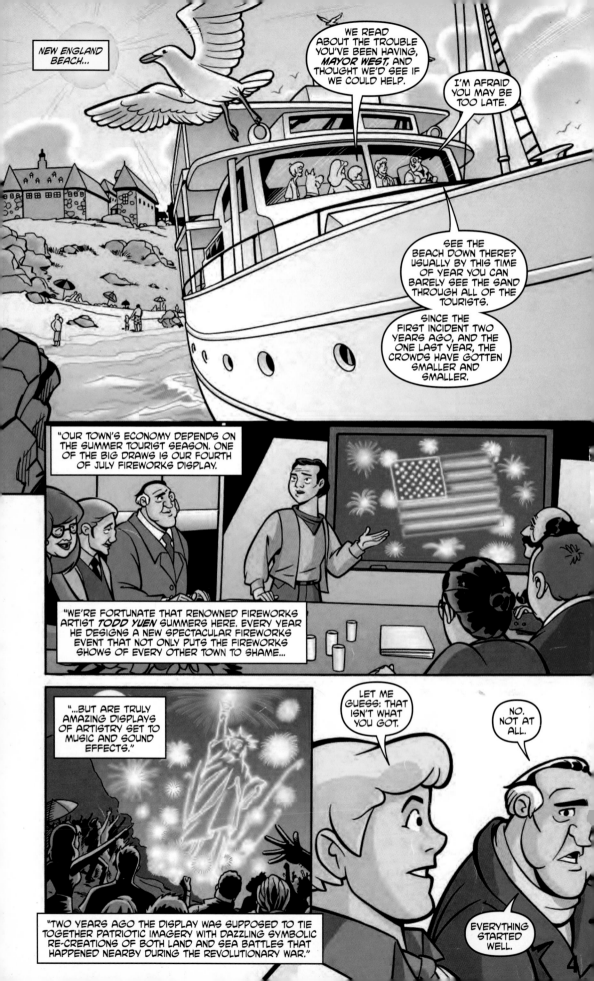

THEN, JUST LIKE *THAT...*

SNAP

...THE CREATURE WAS *GONE.* UNTIL LAST YEAR, ANYWAY.

YOU DID NOT HEED MY WARNING.

I BELIEVE YOU NEED A DEMONSTRATION TO SHOW YOU JUST HOW SERIOUS I AM.

BOOOOM

GASP...

BE GONE! DO NOT HOLD THIS CEREMONY AGAIN, OR NEXT TIME THE ENTIRE TOWN WILL BURN!

NOW TOURISTS ARE STAYING AWAY. THE TOWN COUNCIL WANTS TO CANCEL TONIGHT'S FIREWORKS SHOW. I UNDERSTAND THEIR CONCERNS, BUT I'M RETIRING AT THE END OF THE SUMMER, AND TOLD MYSELF I'D LEAVE THIS TOWN IN BETTER SHAPE THAN IT WAS WHEN I TOOK OFFICE.

YOU'RE GOING THROUGH WITH IT?

I HAVE A PLAN.

I DON'T BELIEVE IN MONSTERS. I THINK THIS IS THE WORK OF SABOTEURS. IF THEY CAN'T GET TO THE FIREWORKS, THEY CAN'T SABOTAGE THEM.

WE LAUNCH THE FIREWORKS FROM THAT BOAT UP AHEAD. ONLY THIS YEAR'S FIREWORKS ARE STOWED SAFELY ON ANOTHER BOAT. WE'RE USING THIS ONE AS A *TRAP.*

WE'LL DO EVERYTHING WE CAN TO HELP SOLVE THIS MYSTERY, BUT IT MIGHT HELP IF WE HAD SOMETHING ELSE TO GO ON.

YOU MIGHT KEEP AN EYE OUT FOR THE GHOSTS.

I MIGHT HAVE KNOWN.

GHOSTS?

EACH YEAR WE'VE HAD THIS PROBLEM. TWO BRITISH RED-COATS SOLDIERS ARE OFTEN SPOTTED SNEAKING AROUND THE WATERFRONT AREA.

THEY USUALLY APPEAR BEGINNING ON JULY FIRST.

LET ME GUESS. THEY'RE BACK.

YES. I'M NOT SURE HOW THEY'RE CONNECTED, BUT IT MIGHT BE WORTH LOOKING INTO.

BUT WHAT MAKES YOU THINK THEY'RE GHOSTS?

BECAUSE THEY APPEAR AND VANISH AT WILL.

OKAY, GANG. LET'S HEAD BACK TO SHORE.

IT'S TIME FOR US TO SPLIT UP. VELMA, YOU, SHAGGY, AND SCOOBY LOOK INTO THESE GHOSTS.

"DAPHNE AND I WILL PAY A VISIT TO TODD YUEN."

WHILE I APPRECIATE YOUR INTEREST IN THE MATTER, I FEAR YOU MAY BE TOO LATE TO BENEFIT ME, ANYWAY.

NOT ONLY DO I PUT ON THE FIREWORKS SHOW HERE EACH SUMMER, BUT I'VE ALSO DESIGNED FIREWORKS SHOWS FOR THE WHITE HOUSE, THEME PARKS, THE OLYMPIC GAMES, SPECIAL ANNIVERSARY EVENTS, AND SPORTING EVENTS.

WHAT'S HAPPENING HERE IS DAMAGING MY REPUTATION.

IS THAT WHY YOU HAVE ALL OF THESE REAL ESTATE FLYERS? ARE YOU THINKING OF MOVING AWAY?

YES. I HAVE A CONTRACT WITH THE TOWN, BUT THE MAYOR TELLS ME THE TOWN COUNCIL WANTS TO CANCEL IT. I'M AFRAID THAT PERSONAL SHAME OVERSHADOWS MY DESIRE TO REMAIN HERE.

SOMETIMES THE NEXT TOWN IS FAR ENOUGH AWAY.

IF YOU'LL EXCUSE ME, I NEED TO GET READY FOR TONIGHT. WISH ME LUCK.

OF COURSE, MR. YUEN.

SOMETHING ISN'T RIGHT HERE, AND I THINK WE'LL FIND THE ANSWERS AT MR. YUEN'S REALTOR. THANKFULL NO REALTOR I'VE EVER HEARD OF TAKES THE DAY OFF FROM WORK, EVEN AN OFFICIAL HOLIDAY.

THESE ARE ALL FOR COMMERCIAL PROPERTIES IN SEASIDE BLUFFS. THAT'S JUST A FEW MILES UP THE COAST. FORGIVE ME, BUT IT HARDLY SEEMS THAT YOU ARE FLEEING IN SHAME. IF YOU'RE JUST MOVING TO THE NEXT TOWN.

DON'T WORRY, WE'LL THINK OF SOME WAY TO SAVE TONIGHT'S SHOW.

WE SHALL SEE.

"HOW DO YOU THINK THE OTHERS ARE DOING?"

OH, MAN, VELMA, LIKE, COULDN'T WE TAKE A BREAK TO FIND OUT IF ANY OF THOSE FRIED CLAM STRIPS TASTE AS GOOD AS THEY SMELL?

THOSE CLAMS AREN'T THE ONLY THINGS THAT SMELL FISHY AROUND HERE, SHAGGY, AND SO FAR WE HAVEN'T FOUND A SINGLE CLUE.

LIKE, HOW'S THIS FOR A CLUE?

CHECK OUT THAT KOOKY FOG BANK THAT'S ONLY CLINGING TO JUST THOSE TWO BOATS.

THAT'S NOT ALL. THERE'S OUR RED-COATS CLIMBING INTO THAT ROW BOAT.

I THINK WE'D BETTER GO SEE WHAT THEY WERE DOING.

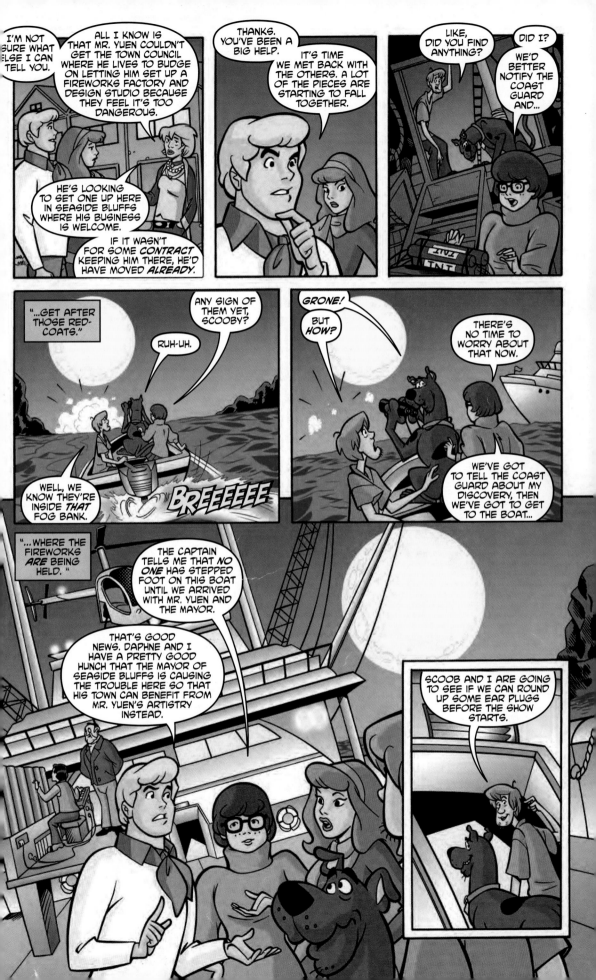

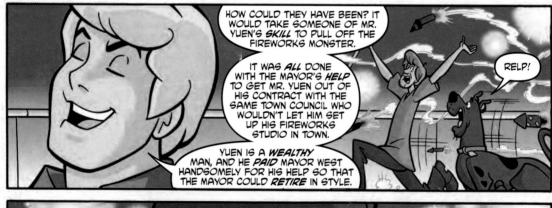